BE SURE TO PRAY, ZAIN!

GREEN KEY PRESS

Be Sure to Pray, Zain!

Written by Humera Malik

First edition

© Green Key Press 2020

A publication of:

Green Key Press
Washington, DC

For further information please visit www.greenkeypress.com.

ISBN 978-0-9989782-4-6

10 9 8 7 6 5 4 3 2 1

Recite that which has been revealed to you of the Book, and observe prayer. Surely prayer restrains one from indecency and manifest evil; and remembrance of Allah, indeed, is the greatest virtue. And Allah knows what you do.

–Holy Quran, 29:46

My Week

I have **NOT** had a good week! Nothing has gone my way. My tutor picked on me at math club and my friends haven't been nice to me.

But I should start by introducing myself.

I'm Zain. I live with my parents, I like to bake with my mom, and build things with my dad. Right now, we are working on a spaceship that we are building out of carboard boxes. It's going to be a-w-e-s-o-m-e!

I am a Muslim, and now that I am growing up I pray five times a day. Well, I am *meant* to pray five times a day—and I really want to, because praying is actually pretty cool. You can ask God for anything! But sometimes I get lazy or forget.

Let's rewind to Sunday night so I can tell you about my terrible week.

Monday

On Monday morning I was having the best dream. So I guess my week didn't start out bad. It's just that, sometimes, when I feel mad, I can only see all the bad things that are happening. Does that ever happen to you? It turns out, my tutor *didn't* pick on me, because I did misbehave a little.

Anyway, back to my dream. I was playing soccer in a huge stadium and the crowd was chanting my name.

Go Zain go! Go Zain go!

That's when my mom came in to wake me for Fajr prayer.

"I don't want to pray, I want to stay in bed," I said, hoping to get back to my dream.

"But Zain," said Mom, "offering your prayers

is the most important thing you do all day."

"Why?", I asked.

Mom replied, "Praying protects us from bad decisions throughout the day."

So I got out of bed, did my ablutions, and went downstairs to pray with Mom and Dad.

"Zain," said Dad, as I stepped onto the prayer rug, "when you pray, you can speak with God and ask him for anything you want."

It was our spelling test at school that day so I prayed that I would ace it. Then I got ready for school, had breakfast, and waited for the school bus.

At school, when it was time for the test, I said Bismillah and I tried my best. At the end of the day, the teacher gave me my test paper back, and I was so happy: I got an A+!

Tuesday

So you see, Monday was a good day. And now that I think about it, Tuesday was kind of awesome too!

After school on Tuesday, I prayed Zuhr with Mom. Then I went to the park to play with some friends. When I got there I saw two boys from the fifth grade picking on my neighbor, Joey. I've seen these boys around school. They are big and behave meanly to a lot of the younger kids.

The boys yanked Joey's bag out of his hands and threw it in a muddy puddle. I quickly ran to Joey and told the older boys to leave him alone.

I was shaking because these boys are much bigger than me, but after a minute they laughed and then they walked away. Phew! Joey and I walked home together after that, because I wanted to make sure he didn't run into those boys again.

In the evening the doorbell rang. Dad went to see who it was, it was Joey and his parents. Joey had told them what happened at the park and they had come to tell my parents and thank me. All the adults were so pleased with me that they decided to take Joey and me out for ice cream. I got a triple scoop of chocolate chocolate chocolate chip!

Wednesday

Wednesday started off great. I had Gym, Art, and Math at school. Those are my favorite subjects. When I got home, Mom was in the kitchen, reading a recipe for blueberry muffins.

"I think we have all the ingredients to make these Zain, would you like to do some baking?", she asked.

"Sure!", I said. So that's what we did.

When the muffins were baking in the oven they smelled **so good!**

"Why don't you change your clothes and offer Asr prayer while the muffins cool, then you can take them to Ali's house," Mom said to me.

So I ran upstairs, quickly got changed and ran back downstairs. You know, now that I

think about it, I forgot to offer Asr that day—
whoops!

"Take the safe route, Zain" said Mom, handing me the muffins to put in my backpack.

Ali lives just two blocks away and there's a path through the park to get to his house. But there's also a shorter way to get there. You have to cross a busy street, so I'm not allowed to go that way. But on that day, I could see that there were no cars coming, so I quickly crossed over.

When I got to Ali's house, I took off my backpack to get the muffins. That's when I saw my bag was wide open and the muffins were not in there. They must have fallen out when I ran to cross the street! I was so disappointed, I had been looking forward to eating them. And to make things even worse, Ali's mom gave us apple slices and carrot sticks for a snack—I hate carrots!

Thursday

Wednesday was a bad day, but Thursday was even worse! School was okay, I guess. I finished my homework, and while Mom made dinner, I read a book. There was a knock on the door. It was Ali and some of my other friends. They were going to play soccer and they invited me along.

"It's nearly time for Maghrib prayer, Zain," Mom reminded me. I knew she would tell me to wait ten minutes so that we could pray together and then I could go to play soccer. But I didn't want to wait so I pretended not to hear her and shouted goodbye as I ran out of the house.

At the park, my friend Tom passed me the ball and I started running towards the goal.

Suddenly, a boy from the other team stole the ball from me. I was **SO mad!** I was about to score a goal and now the other team had the ball. I ran to catch up with the boy and kicked him in the shin. The boy fell down, crying in pain and the other boys stopped playing to help him. The game was over.

I picked up my things and walked home. Once I calmed down, I started to feel bad about what I had done. It looked like that other boy's leg was really hurting. I wish I hadn't got mad and kicked him.

Friday

On Friday evenings, I go to Math Club after dinner.

"Zain, please offer your Isha prayer," said Mom. "Your Dad will be home soon and then he will take you to your class."

But I was busy watching television and I didn't want to miss the end of my show. I will pray after the show finishes, I thought to myself. But before I knew it, I heard Dad's car in the driveway, so I grabbed my bag and went outside.

When I got to the classroom, our tutor told us that we were going to have a multiplication test. I had forgotten all about it and had not learned my times tables! **N-o-o-o-o-o!** Then, I realized I could see Noor's answers. Noor always studied and got good grades, so I

quickly copied down what she had written. At the end of math club, when the tutor returned our test papers, I saw that she had written on my paper in angry red letters: *"SEE ME."*

Gulp. Slowly, I walked to her desk. "Zain, I saw you copying Noor's test, and I am very disappointed in you," she said. "Next week you will have to retake the test."

"Okay," I said, quietly, looking down at my shoes in embarrassment.

And that brings us to this moment. I'm sitting on my bed feeling sad and pretty mad. And I don't know how to make things better.

Still Friday...

"Zain, it's time for dinner," Mom called. I stood up slowly and made my way downstairs. Mom could see I was upset and she asked me if there was anything I wanted to talk about. I looked up, and suddenly, there were tears in my eyes.

I told my parents about all the things that had gone wrong. I told them about the lost muffins that I had been looking forward to eating, that my friends stopped playing soccer with me because I kicked one of the other boys, and that I had cheated on my test and the tutor was angry with me.

Mom asked if I knew why these things might have happened and I said no.

"Zain," said Mom, "have you been offering

your prayers?" I looked away and sadly shook my head, remembering how I had missed a prayer on Wednesday and Thursday and had not read Isha today either.

"Do you remember what I told you about Salat?," she asked.

With a sigh, I replied, "It's the most important thing you can do all day."

"Right," said Mom, "because it protects us from doing bad things."

"How?" I asked.

Mom explained: "Imagine that each of us has a wall around us that is built out of bricks. Our wall blocks bad ideas, making it easier for us to do good things. We get a brick for every prayer we offer. If we pray regularly, we get a lot of bricks so our wall becomes tall and strong. That means it is very hard for bad ideas to get to us."

"But when we miss a prayer, a brick from our wall falls out. You missed three prayers this week and this made a little hole in your wall. Some small, bad ideas snuck in through

the hole and reached you."

"Oh no!", I said, "What should I do now?"

Dad said, "You can mend your wall by offering your prayers five times a day. The hole will be filled with new bricks and you will continue to make your wall bigger and stronger. This way, it will be very hard for bad ideas to get to you."

"Then that is what I will do, inshallah!", I said, getting up from the table and running upstairs to pray Isha and get ready for bed.

Smiling, Mom and Dad followed me up to say goodnight.

Before Dad switched off the light, he said, "Don't forget that when you pray, you can speak with Allah and ask him for anything. You can even ask him to help you win your soccer games! God loves you very much and He loves to answer your prayers."

I closed my eyes feeling happy. I now knew how I could fix my mistake.

Saturday

The next morning, Dad opened my bedroom door, saying, "Zain, it's time to wake up for prayer." But then he stopped. Because I was already awake. In fact, I was already out of bed and offering my prayers.

Today is going to be a good day, inshallah!

Author Acknowledgements

I would like to thank all the scholars and elders who reviewed my manuscript and gave me guidance. Thank you also to my publisher for all their work in making this book a reality. I drafted all the art for this early reader, which Indonesian graphics artist Gonmuki transformed into the beautiful illustrations you see throughout. Thank you to budding illustrators Kashifa and Asifah Mirza for putting the final touches on a number of illustrations, including the cover.

–Humera Malik
Instagram: @booksforlittlemuslims